T0333558

CAROL ANN DUFFY lives in Manchester, where she is
Professor and Creative Director of the Writing School at Manchester
Metropolitan University. She has written for both children and adults,
and her poetry has received many awards, including the Signal Prize for
Children's Verse, the Whitbread, Forward and T. S. Eliot Prizes, and
the Lannan and E. M. Forster Prize in America. She was appointed Poet
Laureate in 2009. In 2011 *The Bees* won the Costa Poetry Award,
and in 2012 she won the PEN Pinter Prize. She was
appointed DBE in 2015.

Christmas Poems

CAROL ANN DUFFY

PICADOR

First published 2021 by Picador
an imprint of Pan Macmillan
The Smithson, 6 Briset Street, London EC1M 5NR
EU representative: Macmillan Publishers Ireland Ltd,
1st Floor, The Liffey Trust Centre, 117–126 Sheriff Street Upper, Dublin 1 D01 YC43
Associated companies throughout the world
www.panmacmillan.com

ISBN 978-1-5290-3874-3

Contents

CHRISTMAS
POEMS

MRS
SCROOGE

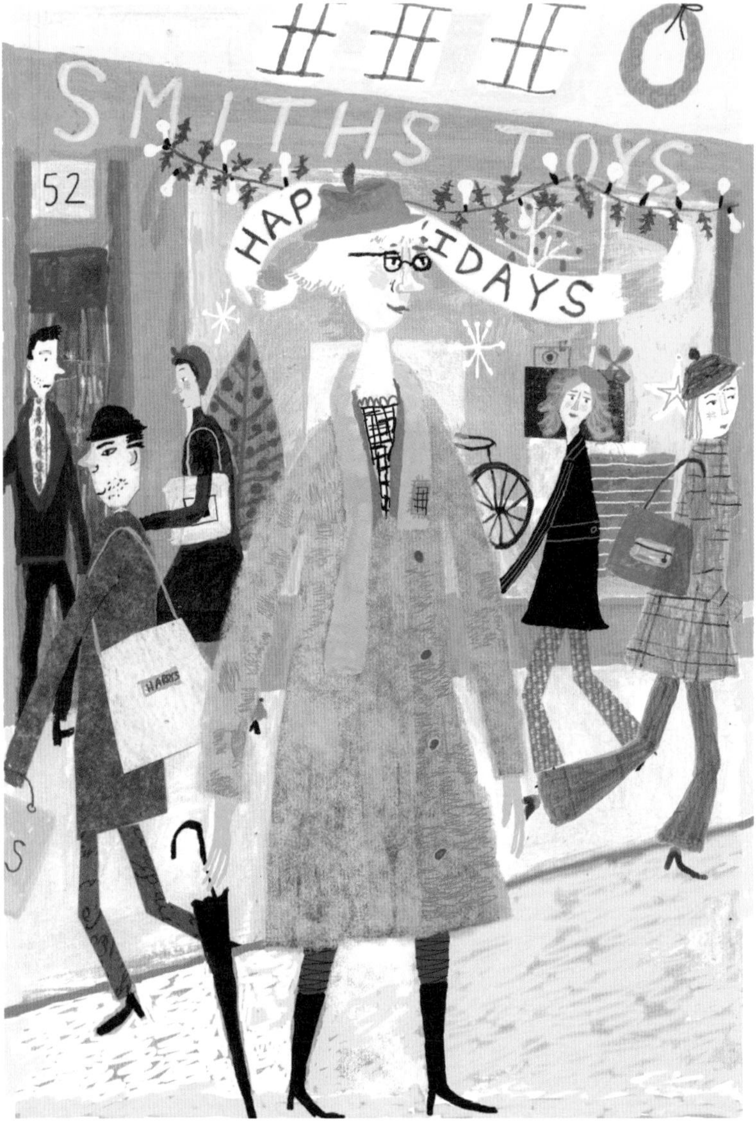
SMITHS TOYS
52
HAP
IDAYS

Scrooge doornail-dead, his widow, Mrs Scrooge, lived by herself
in London Town. It was that time of year, the clocks long back,
when shops were window-dressed with unsold tinsel, trinkets, toys,
trivial pursuits, with sequinned dresses and designer suits,
with chocolates, glacé fruits and marzipan, with Barbie,
Action Man, with bubblebath and aftershave and showergel;
the words *Noël* and *Season's Greetings* brightly mute
in neon lights. The city bells had only just chimed three,
but it was dusk already. It had not been light all day.

Mrs Scrooge sat googling at her desk,

                               Catchit the cat

curled at her feet; snowflakes tumbling to the ground

below the window, where a robin perched,

pecking at seeds. *Most turkeys,*

bred for their meat, are kept in windowless barns,

with some containing over 20,000 birds. Turkeys

are removed from their crates and hung from shackles

by their legs in moving lines. A small fire crackled

in the grate. *Their heads are dragged under*

a water bath – electrically charged – before their necks

are cut. Mrs Scrooge pressed *Print.*

                               She planned

to visit Marley's Supermarket *(Biggest Bargain Birds!)* at four.

12

Outside, snowier yet, and cold! Piercing, searching, biting cold.
The cold gnawed noses just as dogs gnaw bones. It iced
the mobile phones pressed tight to ears.

                                The coldest Christmas Eve
in years saw Mrs Scrooge at Marley's, handing leaflets out.
The shoppers staggered past, weighed down with bags
or pushing trolleys crammed with breasts, legs, crowns, eggs,
sausages, giant stalks of brussels sprouts, carrots,
spuds, bouquets of broccoli, mange tout, courgettes, petits
pois, foie gras; with salmon, Stilton, pork pies, mince pies,
Christmas Pudding, custard,
port, gin, sherry, whisky,
fizz and plonk,
             all done on credit cards.

Most shook their head at Mrs Scrooge,
irked by her cry *"Find out how turkeys really die!"*
or shoved her leaflet in the pockets of their coats, unread,
or laughed and called back, *"Spoilsport! Ho! Ho! Ho!"*
Three hours went by like this.
                          The snow

                                    began to ease

as she walked home.

She hated waste, consumerism, Mrs Scrooge, foraged
in the London parks for chestnuts, mushrooms, blackberries,
ate leftovers, recycled, mended, passed on, purchased secondhand,
turned the heating down and put on layers, walked everywhere,
drank tap-water, used public libraries, possessed a wind-up radio,
switched off lights, lit candles (darkness is cheap and Mrs Scrooge
liked it) and would not spend *one penny* on a plastic bag.
She passed off-licences with *6 for 5*, bookshops with *3 for 2*,
food stores with *Buy 1 get 1 free*.

                                Above her head,
the Christmas lights

                danced like a river toward a sea of dark.
The National Power Grid moaned, endangered, like a whale.

The Thames flowed on as Mrs Scrooge proceeded on her way
towards her rooms.
                                Nobody lived in the building now
but her, and all the other flats were boarded up.
Whatever the developers had offered Mrs Scrooge to move
could never be enough. She liked it where it was,
lurking in the corner of a yard, as though the house
had run there young, playing hide-and-seek,
and had forgotten the way out. She remembered
her first Christmas there with Scrooge,
                                the single stripey sweet
he'd given her that year, and every year.

But Scrooge was dead, no doubt of that, so why,
her key turning the lock, did she see in the knocker
Scrooge's face? His face to the life, staring back at her
with living grey-green eyes and opening metal lips!
As Mrs Scrooge looked fixedly at this,
it turned into a knocker once again.

Up the echoing stairs
to slippers, simple supper, candles, cocoa, cat,
went Mrs Scrooge; not scared, but oddly comforted
at glimpsing Scrooge's knockered face.
But still, she double-locked the door, put on her dressing gown
and sat down by the fire to sip her soup.
                                    The fire
was very low indeed, not much on such a bitter night,
so soon enough she went to bed – night-cap, bed-socks,
Scrooge's old pyjamas, hot-water bottle, Catchit's purr . . .
and then her own soft snore.

She dreamed of Scrooge,

of Christmas past,

of Christmas present, Christmas yet to come; dreams
that seemed to trap her in a snowstorm bowl –
newly-married, ice-skating with Scrooge,
two necks in one long, bright red, woolly scarf;
or hanging baubles on the tree;
or being surprised by mistletoe, his kiss, the taste of him –
but then her world was shaken violently
and she was kneeling by a grave, hearing a funeral bell . . .

Midnight rang out from St Paul's. She gasped awake.
The twice-locked door was open wide
and all the room was filled with light
and smelled of tangerines and cinnamon and wine.
A cheerful Ghost was perched and grinning on her bed,
now like a child, now like a wise old man,
with silver hair and berried holly for a crown
(and yet its shimmering dress was trimmed with flowers).
"*Good grief!*" said Mrs Scrooge. "*Who the hell are you?*"
The Ghost squealed with delight and clapped its hands
(a hard thing for a ghost to do, thought Mrs Scrooge).
"*I am the Ghost of Christmas Past,*" it trilled.
"*Now, rise! And walk with me.*"

It took her by the hand
then flew her through the bedroom wall. They stood at once
upon an open country road, with fields on either side.
The city had entirely gone, the darkness too;
it was a sparkling winter's day, all blinged with frost.
"I know this place!" cried Mrs Scrooge. *"I grew up here!*
We're near the village of Heath Row!
My family kept an orchard close to here."
They walked along the road, Mrs Scrooge recalling
every gate, and post, and tree.

"*T*hat way's Harmondsworth,"
she told the Ghost excitedly. "*Famous for Richard Cox,*
you know, who cultivated Cox's Orange Pippin."
The merry Ghost conjured an apple from the air.
She crunched delightedly. "*That way's Longford village;*
that way's the farm at Perry Oaks; and that way's Sipson Green!"
They'd reached the village now, a green, a row of houses and an Inn;
two fields away a farm, beyond that farm another farm;
the landscape glittering as if it were in love with light.
A laughing local bunch of lads ran by.
Mrs Scrooge went red!
"*I snogged that tall one once!*" she said.

"*They're shadows,*"
said the Ghost. "*They have no consciousness of us.*"
High in the sky there came an aeroplane, rare enough
to make the boys stand pointing at the endless, generous air
and yell out "*Merry Christmas!*" to the plane.

"*This is the past,
it cannot come again,*" went on the Ghost, "*It is the gift
your soul gives to your heart.*"
Mrs Scrooge stopped in the road and turned. "*Why show
me this?*" she asked. "*Because,*" the Ghost replied,
"*Scrooge sends a message from the grave –
keep going! You shall overcome!*"
"*No Runway Three!*" cried Mrs Scrooge,
the breath her words made
like a ghost itself, swooning, vanishing.

But when she looked,
the face of Christmas Past bent down,
just like a lover stoops to steal a kiss,
and then her lips were soft, then salty,
tasting tears, her own, and then she woke,
at home, and old, and all alone.

Not quite alone,
for Catchit dozed and snuggled at her feet,
visions of robin redbreasts in his head.

London's moon,
the moon of Shakespeare, Dickens, Oscar, Virginia Woolf,
shone down on silent theatres, banks, hotels,
on palaces and dosshouses and parks,

on Mrs Scrooge,
who lay, wide-eyed and fretful, in the dark. She heard
a scrabbling noise inside the chimney-breast
and sat bolt upright in her bed —

"Who's there?" she said —
then, with a thump, a flash,

a figure in a crimson Santa suit
glowed in the grate, as if the fire had taken human shape
and combed itself a beard from its smoke.
"I am the Ghost of Christmas Present,"
boomed the Ghost. *"Now rise, and come with me!"*

Before she knew it, Mrs Scrooge sat in a sleigh,
being pulled by reindeers through the starry sky,
tying a ribbon round the earth;
the Ghost of Christmas Present talking as they flew, naming
the oceans, forests, mountain ranges far below,
until the Arctic Circle rose beneath them like a moon.
They landed,
                    skidding on the ice,
in a percussion of sharp hooves and jingling bells.

Tears, like opals,
                    fell, then froze,
on Mrs Scrooge's cheeks as she looked.
She stood upon a continent of ice
which sparkled between sea and sky,
                                        endless and dazzling,
as though the world kept all its treasure there;
                                        a scale
which balanced poetry and prayer.

But then she heard a crackling, rumbling groan
and saw huge icebergs calving from the floe

                              into the sea;
then, further out, a polar bear, floating,

                              stranded,
on a raft of ice.
                    "The Polar Ice Cap melting," said the Ghost.
"Can mankind save it?"
"Yes, we can!" cried Mrs Scrooge. *"We must!"*
"I bring encouragement from Scrooge's dust," replied the Ghost.
*"Never give up. Don't think one ordinary human life
can make no difference – for it can!"*

The reindeers steamed and snorted in the snow.
Mrs Scrooge stretched out her hand to one,
stroking the warm, rough texture of its hide,
which seemed to alter, soften, into Catchit's fur!
The North Pole vanished like a snuffed-out flame.
She woke again.

"*O*ld fool!"

said Mrs Scrooge to herself. *"These are just dreams."*
She pulled her blankets up beneath her chin
and lay there, worrying about large things and small.
The wall flickered with strange shadows, shifting shapes —
a turkey, and then a bear, and then a hooded form
which pointed at her silently,
until it swelled and stood and spoke!
"I am the Ghost of Christmas Yet to Come! Rise now,
and follow me!"

It took her in its arms like a bride
and flew her through a winter wood
towards a clearing
                    and an open grave,
around which mourners stood,
                              then put her down.
"*My family!*" said Mrs Scrooge. "*There's Bob!*
And that's his lovely wife!
There are my grandchildren! Peter! Martha! Tiny Tim!
Look! They're my dearest friends, the Fezziwigs! Their girls!
Why are we here? Who died?"

The Spirit pointed downward to the grave.
Mrs Scrooge crept near and peeped into a wormy, loamy hole.
She saw a cardboard coffin, crayoned brightly with a name,
cartooned with flowers, faces, animals,
covered with poems, kisses, hearts.

She turned . . .

At once, she stood beside the Ghost
inside a huge and crowded room,
her friends and family piling in!
In came a fiddler with a music-book
who started up a jig.

(Mrs Scrooge,
who loved a whirl,
restrained herself from dancing with the Ghost.)

In came Mrs Fezziwig, one vast substantial smile,
bearing a tray of home-made, warm mince pies; saying
"She would have wanted it this way!" In came
the Fezziwig girls with babies chuckling in their arms. In came
tall nephews arm-in-arm with little aunts.

                              In came old comrades
with whom she'd marched in protest
against every kind of harm.
                    In they all came,
aglow with life and possibility, old and young;
away they went, twenty couples all at once,
gay and straight, down the middle, up and round again,
the beaming fiddler trying to saw his instrument in half!

There never was

        such a wake!

More dancing, then more music, someone sang,

several shed tears;

then mince pies, cake, mulled wine, cold beer,

more wine, more beer;

then Mrs Scrooge heard a cheer

and there was Tiny Tim, up on a chair!

There was a hush.

        "A toast!"

cried Tiny Tim. *"To my grandmother! The best woman*

who ever was! She taught us all

to value everything!

        To give ourselves!

To live as if each day

        was Christmas Day!"

Another cheer and Mrs Scrooge's name rang out
from everybody's lips.
                              She seemed to float
above them; all the bright, familiar faces
                                        looking up,
raised glasses in the air.
She heard Bob say, *"She really had a wonderful life!"*
The Ghost of Christmas Yet to Come
                                    pulled back its hood.
She looked into its smiling, loving, grey-green eyes
and understood.

Clash, clang, hammer, ding, dong, bell!
Bell, dong, ding, hammer, clang, clash!
It was St Paul's again,
            gargling its morning bells,
the room her own;
            and dribbling Catchit
staring down at her from her chest!
Quickly, Mrs Scrooge showered and dressed.
She flung open the window and leaned out —
a clear, bright, jovial, cold and glorious day!

The doorbell rang.
              Down she hurried,
opened wide the door,
                    and in they poured,
taking the stairs two at a time – Bob, Bob's wife,
the grandchildren, the Fezziwigs,
their girls, babies, partners,
                    all shouting
"Merry Christmas! Merry Christmas! Merry Christmas!"

W hat news they had!

     The credit crunch
had forced the property developers
to sell the empty flats below to the Fezziwig girls!
So come New Year, all three were moving in!
Hurrah! Hurrah! What did Mrs Scrooge think of *that*!
(And would she babysit?)

       Bob came grinning from the kitchen
with a tray of glasses of Buck's Fizz!
Mrs Fezziwig and Mrs Scrooge

      cuddled and wept with joy!
And that delightful boy, Tiny Tim, called out,
*"Here you are, Grandma, the sweet that Grandad gave you
every Christmas that he lived! A . . ."*

      "HUMBUG!"

exclaimed Mrs Scrooge!
"God Bless Us, Every One!" cried Tiny Tim.

ANOTHER
NIGHT BEFORE
CHRISTMAS

On the night before Christmas, a child in a house,
As the whole family slept, behaved just like a mouse . . .
And crept on soft toes down red-carpeted stairs.
Her hand held the paw of her favourite bear.

The Christmas tree posed with its lights in its arms,
Newly tinselled and baubled with glittering charms;
Flirting in flickers of crimson and green
Against the dull glass of the mute TV screen.

The hushed street was in darkness. Snow duveted the cars –
A stray cat had embroidered each roof with its paws.
An owl on an aerial had planets for eyes.
The child at the window stared up at the sky,

Where two aeroplanes sped to the east and the west,
Like a pulled Christmas cracker. The child held her breath
And looked for a sign up above, as the moon
Shone down like a gold chocolate coin on the town.

Far beyond the quiet suburbs, the motorway droned
As it cradled the drivers who murmured at phones
And drove through the small hours, this late Christmas Eve,
The ones who were faithless, the ones who believed.

But the child who was up and long out of her bed
Saw no visions of sugar plums dance in her head;
She planned to discover, for once and for all,
If Santa Claus (or Father Christmas) was real.

There were some who said no, he was really just Mum,
With big cushions or pillows to plump out her tum,
Or Dad, with a red cloak and cotton-wool beard,
A whisky or three down his neck for Good Cheer.

So she took up position behind a big chair
That was close to the fireplace. Four stockings hung there.
Quite soon there'd be one tangerine in each toe
And she'd be the child who would see and would know.

And outside, a lone taxi crunched back into town,
Where the shops had their shutters, like giant eyelids, down,
And people in blankets, with nowhere to go,
Were hunched in shop doorways to keep from the snow;

Where a giant plastic Santa climbed up the Town Hall
And security guards dozed or smoked in the Mall.
The cashpoints glowed softly, like icons of light,
From corner to corner, on Christmas Eve night.

Then a shooting star whizzed down the sky from the North.
It was fizzing and sparkling as it fell to earth,
And growing in size. A young hare in a field
Gazed up at the sky where it brightened and swelled.

It turned into a sleigh, made of silver and gold,
Pulled by reindeer, whose breath chiffoned out in the cold,
With bells on their antlers and bells round each hoof.
Then – clatter! – they landed on you-know-who's roof.

Now, herself near the fireplace had fallen asleep,
So she missed every word that a voice, warm and deep,
Was saying above her, as each reindeer's name
Was spoken, and flared in the night like a flame.

Dasher, whoa! Dancer, whoa! Prancer! Vixen! Well done!
Comet, whoa! Cupid, whoa! Donner! Blitzen! What fun!
The shadows of reindeer were patterns on snow
Which gift-wrapped the garden, three storeys below.

It's a fact that a faraway satellite dish,
Which observes us from space, cannot know what we wish.
Its eye's empty socket films famine and greed,
But cannot see Santa Claus on Christmas Eve.

He was dressed all in red, from his head to his toes,
Also red was the Christmassy glow of his nose.
His beard was as white as the flakes that fell down
On rich and on poor in this ordinary town.

His eyes twinkled like tinsel and starlight and frost,
And they knew how to give without counting the cost.
He'd slung on his back a huge sackful of toys
To lug down the chimneys of good girls and boys.

Dasher snorted, and Blixen pawed hard at the roof –
They'd a long night before them, and that was the truth!
But Santa had vanished! A puff of black soot
Burped out of the chimney, dislodged by his foot.

All this noise woke the child, who had fallen asleep,
So she popped up her head and made sure she could peep
(Without being seen) at whoever it was
Who stood in the fireplace. Big Wow! Santa Claus!

Though she lived in an age where celebrity ruled
And when most of the people were easily fooled
By TV and fashion, by money and cars,
The little girl knew that here was a real STAR!

Then she watched as the room filled with magic and light
As the spirit of Christmas made everything bright
And suddenly presents were heaped by the tree —
But she didn't wonder, which ones are for me?

For the best gift of all is to truly believe
In the wonderful night that we call Christmas Eve,
When adults remember, of all childhood's laws,
This time in December will bring Santa Claus.

Santa turned and he winked at her, then disappeared,
With a laugh, up the chimney, with soot in his beard.
She ran to the window and watched as his sleigh
Took off from her roof and he sped on his way.

And as long as she lived she would never forget
How he flew, as the moon showed him in silhouette,
From rooftop to rooftop and called from his flight
HAPPY CHRISTMAS TO ALL
    AND TO ALL A GOOD NIGHT.

THE
CHRISTMAS
TRUCE

Christmas Eve in the trenches of France,
the guns were quiet.
The dead lay still in No Man's Land –
Freddie, Franz, Friedrich, Frank . . .
The moon, like a medal, hung in the clear, cold sky.

Silver frost on barbed wire, strange tinsel,
sparkled and winked.
A boy from Stroud stared at a star
to meet his mother's eyesight there.
An owl swooped on a rat on the glove of a corpse.

In a copse of trees behind the lines,
a lone bird sang.
A soldier-poet noted it down – *a robin*
holding his winter ground –
then silence spread and touched each man like a hand.

Somebody kissed the gold of his ring;
a few lit pipes;
most, in their greatcoats, huddled,
waiting for sleep.
The liquid mud had hardened at last in the freeze.

But it was Christmas Eve; *believe*; belief
thrilled the night air,
where glittering rime on unburied sons
treasured their stiff hair.
The sharp, clean, midwinter smell held memory.

On watch, a rifleman scoured the terrain –
no sign of life,
no shadows, shots from snipers,
nowt to note or report.
The frozen, foreign fields were acres of pain.

T hen flickering flames from the other side
danced in his eyes,
as Christmas Trees in their dozens shone,
candlelit on the parapets,
and they started to sing, all down the German lines.

M en who would drown in mud, be gassed, or shot,
or vaporised
by falling shells, or live to tell,
heard for the first time then –
Stille Nacht. Heilige Nacht. Alles schläft, einsam wacht . . .

Cariad, the song was a sudden bridge
from man to man;
a gift to the heart from home,
or childhood, some place shared . . .
When it was done, the British soldiers cheered.

A Scotsman started to bawl *The First Noel*
and all joined in,
till the Germans stood, seeing
across the divide,
the sprawled, mute shapes of those who had died.

All night, along the Western Front, they sang,
the enemies —
carols, hymns, folk songs, anthems,
in German, English, French;
each battalion choired in its grim trench.

So Christmas dawned, wrapped in mist,
to open itself
and offer the day like a gift
for Harry, Hugo, Hermann, Henry, Heinz . . .
with whistles, waves, cheers, shouts, laughs.

Frohe Weihnachten, Tommy! Merry Christmas, Fritz!
A young Berliner,
brandishing schnapps,
was the first from his ditch to climb.
A Shropshire lad ran at him like a rhyme.

Then it was up and over, every man,
to shake the hand
of a foe as a friend,
or slap his back like a brother would;
exchanging gifts of biscuits, tea, Maconochie's stew,

Tickler's jam . . . for cognac, sausages, cigars,
beer, sauerkraut;
or chase six hares, who jumped
from a cabbage-patch, or find a ball
and make of a battleground a football pitch.

I showed him a picture of my wife.
Ich zeigte ihm
ein Foto meiner Frau.
Sie sei schön, sagte er.
He thought her beautiful, he said.

They buried the dead then, hacked spades
into hard earth
again and again, till a score of men
were at rest, identified, blessed.
Der Herr ist mein Hirt . . . my shepherd, I shall not want.

And all that marvellous, festive day and night,
they came and went,
the officers, the rank and file,
their fallen comrades side by side
beneath the makeshift crosses of midwinter graves . . .

. . . beneath the shivering, shy stars
and the pinned moon
and the yawn of History;
the high, bright bullets
which each man later only aimed at the sky.

WENCESLAS

The King's Cook had cooked for the King
a Christmas Pie,

           wherein the Swan,
once bride of the river,
half of for ever,
six Cygnets circling her,
lay scalded, plucked, boned, parboiled,
salted, peppered, gingered, oiled;

and harboured the Heron
whose grey shadow she'd crossed
as it stood witness,

        grave as a Priest,
on the riverbank.

Now the Heron's breast was martyred with Cloves.

Inside the Heron inside the Swan –
in a greased cradle, pastry-sealed –
a Common Crane,

        gutted and trussed,
smeared with Cicely, Lavender, Rose,
was stuffed with a buttered, saffroned
golden Goose.

Within the Goose,
perfumed with Fruits, was a Duck,
and jammed in the Duck, a Pheasant,
embalmed in Honey

      from Bees

           who'd perused

the blossoms of Cherry trees.

Spring in deep midwinter;

      a year in a pie;

a Guinea-Fowl in a Pheasant;
a Teal in a Fowl.

Nursed in the Teal,
a Partridge, purse to a Plover;
a Plover, glove to a Quail;
and caught in the mitt of the Quail,

                    a Lark —
a green Olive stoppered its beak.

The Christmas Pie
for the good King, Wenceslas,
was seasoned with Sage, Rosemary, Thyme;
and a living Robin sang through a hole in its crust.

Pot-herbs to accompany this;
Roasted Chestnuts, Red Cabbage,
Celery, Carrots, Colly-flowre,
each borne aloft by a Page

                    into the Hall,
where the Pie steamed on a table
in front of the fire;

               and to flow at the feast,
mulled Wine, fragrant
with Nutmeg, Cinnamon, Mace,
with Grains of Paradise.

                   The Lords and Ladies
sat at their places, candlelight
on their festive faces.

Up in the Minstrels' Gallery,
the King's Musicians tuned the Lute
to the Flute
        to the Pipe
to the Shawm, the Gemshorn, the Harp,
to the Dulcimer
        to the Psaltery;
and the Drum was a muffled heart
like an imminent birth
and the Tambourine was percussion as mirth.

Then a blushing Boy stood to trill
of how the Beasts, by some good spell,
in their crude stable began to tell
the gifts they gave Emmanuel.

Holly, Ivy, Mistletoe,

                   shredded Silver,

hung from the rafters
and the King's Fool

                 pranced beneath

five red Apples,

           one green Pear,

which danced in the air.

Snow at the window twirled;
and deep, crisp, even,

                  covered the fields

where a fox and a vixen curled in a den
as the Moon scowled
at the cold, bold, gold glare of an Owl.

Also there,

        out where the frozen stream

lay nailed to the ground,

was a prayer

        drifting as human breath,

as the ghost of words,

        in a dark wood,

yearning to be

      Something

        Understood.

But Heaven was only old light
and the frost was cruel
where a poor, stooped man

went gathering fuel.

A miracle then,

fanfared in,
that the King in red robes, silver crown,
glanced outside

from his wooden throne
to see the Pauper

stumble, shiver,
and sent a Page to fetch him

Hither.

Then Wenceslas sat the poor man down,
poured Winter's Wine,
and carved him a sumptuous slice

of the Christmas Pie . . .

as prayers hope You would, and I.

BETHLEHEM

A mild dusk; the little town
                    snaked
on the edge between desert and farmland;
camel prints in the sand
                    like broken hearts;
the call and response of sheep
                    among dry shrub.

To the West,
          the whispering prayer of olive groves;
incense of rosemary, cedar, pine, votive
on purpling air.

Everyone there who had to be there.

The lamps lit; all Bethlehem
full;
every cave stabled with beasts, jostling for hay
in the fusty gloom;
every room
peopled and packed from rafter to floor;
barley bread in the ovens rising . . .

and a girl's hands
at an open door,
her blade halving a pomegranate,
its blood on her pale palms . . .
a voice from an alleyway chanting a psalm.

The moon rose; the shepherds sprawled,

                                 shawled,

a rough ring on sparse grass, passing
a leather flask.

                From the town,
a swelling human sound; cooking smells braiding the hour
as lambs and fishes spat in the fires.

A hundred suppers —

                    honey, fig, olive, grape,
set before stone-cutter, potter, tent-maker, maid,
nurse, farmer, child.

Young wine in the old jars, yellow and cold.

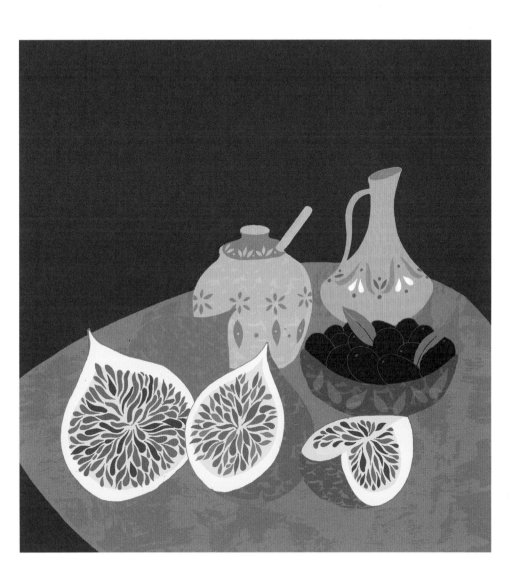

The Inn bulged; travellers boozed,

                        bawled,

bragged, swapping their caravan tales; money-lenders
biting their gold coins;

                  painted women

dancing on tables; mules brayed
outside in the stable;
a youth in the courtyard strummed on a harp.

The sweating Innkeeper shouted and served;
his wife counting the heads,
then making up beds on the flat roof,
in the vine-covered yard.

Above, bright news in the sky, arrived, a star.

The small hours; all living souls

                              slept
or half-slept; the night fires smouldering low
out in the scrub;
the olive oil cooling in clay lamps;
a goatherd snored in the straw

                              between two goats.

Silent night;
           a soft breeze from the desert
laying a dusting of sand on the dark road,
blessing the homes.

A donkey's slow, deliberate hooves on the stones.

Afterwards, the witnesses

                              spoke

of a singing boy, an angel,
walking the fields in the hour before dawn,
winged in his own light;
of how the shepherds fled from the sight,
lambs in their arms.

And some swore, on their lives,
on their children's lives,
that they saw an olive tree

                              turning to pure gold . . .

that the moon stooped low to gape at the world.

W hat's certain – the time and place:

                                  heard,

three crows from the cockerel;

                         seen,

the stable behind the Inn;

                    present,

animals, goatherd, shepherds, Innkeeper, wife . . .
then the small, raw cry of a new life.

And one wept at a miracle; another
was hoping it might be so;
                                others ran,
daft, shouting, to boast in the waking streets.

Wise men swayed on camels out of the East.

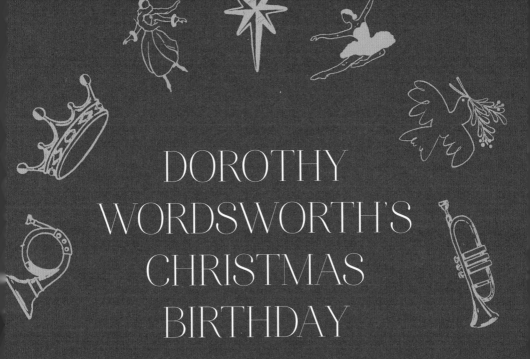

DOROTHY
WORDSWORTH'S
CHRISTMAS
BIRTHDAY

First, frost at midnight –
Moon, Venus and Jupiter
named in their places.

Ice, like a cold key,
turning its lock on the lake;
nervous stars trapped there.

Darkness, a hand poised
over the chord of the hills;
the strange word *moveless*.

The landscape muted;
soft apprehension of snow,
a holding of breath.

Up, rapt at her gate,
Dorothy Wordsworth ages
one year in an hour;

her Christmas birthday
inventoried by an owl,
clock-eyed, time-keeper.

Indoors, the thrilled fire
unwraps itself; sprightly hands
opening the coal.

For she cannot sleep,
Dorothy, primed with herself,
waiting for morning . . .

gradual sure light,
like the start of a poem,
its local accent.

S triding towards dawn,
Samuel Taylor Coleridge
swigs at his port wine,

sings a nonsense rhyme,
which Helm Crag learns and echoes
at the speed of sound.

The rock formations —
old lady at piano,
a lion, a lamb.

And, out on a limb,
he skids down a silvered lane
into a sunburst;

a delight of bells,
the exact mood of his heart,
from St. Oswald's Church.

New rime on the grass
where the Wordsworths' graves will be
at another time.

Not there, then; here, now,
Dorothy's form on the road
coming to meet him,

in her claret frock,
in her boots, bonnet and shawl,
her visible breath.

Then her arms through his
on the stroll to Dove Cottage;
spiced apples baking.

W ordsworth lies a-bed
in his nightshirt and nightcap,
rhyming *cloud* with *crowd*.

The cat at his feet
licks at her black-and-white fur,
rhyming *purr* with *purr*.

The kitchen table,
set for this festive breakfast,
an unseen still-life:

cream in a brown jug,
the calmness of bowls and spoons,
one small round white loaf.

And a tame robin,
aflame on the windowsill,
its name in its song.

They walk to the lake,
where Wordsworth skates like a boy,
in heaven on earth;

a tangerine sun
illuminating the hour
into manuscript;

so Dorothy's gifts
are the gold outlines of hills,
are emblazoned trees;

Coleridge on a rock,
lighting his pipe, votive smoke
ascending the air . . .

Nowt to show more fair –
ecstatic, therefore, her stare,
seeing it all in.

Later, the lamps lit
in the parlour, hot punch fumes
in a copper pan.

The feast: mutton pie,
buttered parsnips, potatoes,
a Halifax goose.

Coleridge's flushed face,
never so vivid again
in Dorothy's mind.

Loud boots at the porch
and a stout thump on the door
as the Minstrels come,

dangling their tin cans
for a free ladle of ale
after caroling . . .

Bring us good ale,
for that goes down at once-oh!
Bring us in good ale . . .

All in each other,
Miss Wordsworth and the poets,
bawling the chorus;

their voices drifting,
in 1799,
to nowhen, nowhere . . .

but Winter's slow turn
and snow in Dorothy's hair
and on her warm tongue.

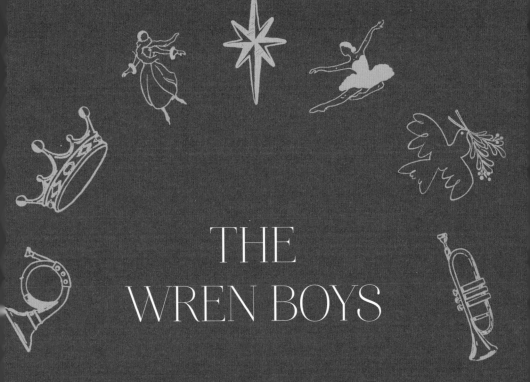

THE
WREN BOYS

The old year, a tear in the eye of time;
frost on the blackthorn, the ditches glamorous
with rime; on the inbreath of air,
the long, thoughtful pause before snow.

A star on the brow of a mule in a field
and the mule nuzzling the drystone wall
where a wren, size of a child's lost purse,
hides in a hole. St. Stephen's Day.

Eight bells from the Church. Next to the Church,
the Inn. Next to the Inn, and opposite,
a straight furlong of dwellings. End of the line,
a farm. Top of the hill, the Big House —

everywhere musky with peat from the first fires
as though the hour had started the day
with a neat malt; like your man has here
who bangs on door after door with his holly-stick.

Quick boys! Up for the wren! Then the Wren-Boys
flinging open the doors in their green-laced boots,
daft caps, red neckerchiefs, with cudgels and nets;
one with a cage held aloft on the tip of a ribboned staff.

Hedge-bandit, song-bomb, dart-beak, the wren
hops in the thicket, flirt-eye; shy, brave,
grubbing, winter's scamp, but more than itself —
ten requisite grams of the world's weight.

And here's the craic: that the little bird
had betrayed a saint with its song,
or stolen a ride on an eagle's back
to fly highest; traitor and cheat.

But poets named it *Dryw*, druid and wren,
sought its hermit tune for a muse;
sweethearts thought it a foolproof blessing for love.
Which was true for the wren? None of the above.

Over the wall, over the field, was the wood
to where the Wren-Boys stomped in a singing gang:
We'll chase him from bush to bush
and from tree to tree. One had a fiddle,

one had a penny-whistle, another a drum,
one had thirty feathers poked in his hat.
So through the holly, the hazel, the ash,
the brackeny floor, they hunted the wren.

Five hours in, they had startled a fox
which ran like the hounds; had bagged a nest
with five blue unhatched eggs; scarpered
from a cache of poteen stashed in an oak.

On a twig, a robin watched them go,
safe in its myth. It had started to snow
and the boots of the boys blotted the page of the field
as they made for the margins – the ditches and hedgerows.

The priest was supping a pint of stout in the pub,
a small icon of his holy self, clocking the top shelf.
The farmer was sat by the fire with his dog.
Four widows were sharing a Christmas nog.

And the sky went falling, falling, down to the earth
till a lad was sent to fetch the mule to its stall,
and the bell had a muffled, sorrowful sound
and up at the Big House all the lights came on.

And the clouds came grieving, grieving, down to the land,
but could they find *that feckin wran,*
as they thrashed, poked, joshed and joked
along the lane where weddings and funerals came.

Who it was who plonked his arse on a stile
and yanked the wipe from his neck, the plumes
from his brother's hat, to fashion a dummy bird,
no living man can tell; nor hear their boisterous glee

as they caged the raggedy wren and swaggered,
whistling, fiddling, drumming, back up the road –
The wren, the wren, the Lord of all birds,
On St. Stephen's Day was caught on the furze . . .

Sing holly, sing ivy, sing ivy, sing holly,
a drop just to drink it will drown melancholy . . .
away round the bend in dwindling violet light
into their given lives, snow-ghosts, gone . . .

to boast at each house with a verse, a sock
for farthings, threepennies, sixpences, florins;
then toast that the wren was out with the old
and in with the new was the robin.

Which would have been news to the wren,
had it understood claptrap, mythology, fable,
warm in its communal roost in the stable
over the heads of the dozing beasts –

while the Wren-Boys boozed and danced at the Inn;
one with a widow, one with the farmer's daughter,
one with a sweetheart, one with a sozzled priest.
Later, the snow settled, a star in the east.

THE KING
OF
CHRISTMAS

Bored, the Baron mooched in his Manor
on the brink of belligerence. Life lacked glamour
and Christmas was coming. The Baroness,
past her best, oozed *ennui*, stitched away
at a tapestry. The old Retainer polished brass.
The Baron felt like kicking his arse.

Outside the leaded window – snow,
snow on snow; the ground an inkless folio.
What to do to enliven life? To put some fizz
on the viz of the wife? Even the hounds,
in a stupor, snored. The son and heir,
party-pooper, piously prone in prayer, as per.

What would the King do? London's Mayor?
Gentry, clergy, artisans, serfs, would soon pitch up
on the Baron's turf; but a gloomy grey, smokey, snide,
drifted, semi-paralysed. The Baron cursed.
Then the Baroness looked up from her crewel,
murmured, 'Appoint a Lord of Misrule.'

Apprentices were poked from straw, lined up,
scratching, in the Hall; alongside yeomen,
glovers, weavers, smiths, brewers, cordwainers . . .
A cake with a buried bean was baked
and he who bit on the bean was booked
as King of Christmas, whose writ ran good.

Now Willie Spear, anarchic fellow, in pantaloons
of violent yellow, had done his share of poaching,
wenching, any villainy you care to mention . . .
and he stuck his tongue – bean-gleam, drool –
in the Baron's face. 'All bow! All kneel! My Lord's a fool!
Twelve days and nights I am Lord of Misrule!'

On the first day of Christmas, William decreed
all labouring men were to lie abed. Wives instead
must enter taverns, mimic slatterns, carouse,
booze, shriek, stagger home, skirts in pleats.
This also applied to the Baroness, who spent
six sick sessions in the same silk dress.

No school for the young. No traitors hung.
No work to be done. No churchbells rung.
Priests were attired in petticoats, pretty ribbons
at their throats. A monkey, dressed in a silver suit,
was served at table in the Baron's seat. Servants walked
upon their hands. And all night long, the pissed Band.

Then William sent out far and wide
to scour the snowy countryside for poets, astrologers,
fools, magicians; gave them all Official Positions,
gorgeous robes, coin-plump purses; commissioned
rude and filthy verses; made No-marks famous;
had the Baron's horoscope cast beneath Uranus.

The Baronial pile was a transformed place. Crazy
candlelight on painted face. The son and heir,
finger-stocked to purge prayer, was squeezed, snogged,
by each lass there. The Baroness, who'd taken to mead,
was ordered to wait on her own maid – *quid pro quo.*
Outside, twelve glovers made a moon of snow.

Regaled by this frenzied Bacchanalia, oxter-deep
in a barrel of ale, the Baron mused.
Up on the flagpole, Will Spear's leggings
kicked at Heaven. On the frozen moat
children skated. In his very own chair, a mangy monkey
masticated. The odds were even, evens odd. Dear God . . .

The Bishop's bottom was being used for Bullseye.
All was mockery, sorcery, debauchery,
anarchy, larceny . . . and yet, the party
had a Yuletide sparkle: every fruit, wrapped
in tinsel; plump geese roasting; marzipan mangers;
everywhere, angels, baubles, candles.

186

Will Spear, too, surveyed the scene, serene
in the pose of a natural leader, enthroned
on the back of a docile donkey, who chomped hay
from the palm of the monkey. Twelfth Night drew near.
Will ordered everyone there to bed; to return by morn
with a sober head. 'Prepare for the final feast,' he said.

Silence fell. Subtle snow. In the arms of a girl, freed
from his stocks, the son and heir smiled in his sleep.
Baron and Baroness, ditto, blotto; a jumbly, fumbly,
marital heap. Masters and servants topped-and-tailed.
Then the snow ceased and the Moon shone down
on its own cold twin, alone on the lawn.

There never was such a spread as Spear supplied,
so legend has it. All day he had them baking,
basting, battering, blanching, boiling, broiling,
carmelizing, chopping, creaming, dicing,
drizzling, filleting, glazing, grating,
grilling, grinding, kneading, mincing, mixing,

peeling, pickling, poaching, rendering, roasting,
scalding, searing, simmering, tossing, trussing,
whipping, till the ancient table groaned and creaked
like the fallen oak of its sylvan past. Then a blast
from a trumpet, each glass filled; the banquet started
at a prompt from the Lord of Misrule. He farted.

And the Baron would remember his laughing wife;
the son and heir marry the love of his life – Amen –
the priest lead everyone across the fields,
when the feast was finished, to church, to kneel,
give thanks, while a boy and a monkey swang
from the bell. And so passed Willie Spear's Noël.

PABLO PICASSO'S NOËL

A sweet winter light blushed
as Pablo Picasso walked with his dog
under the cypress trees
and the bell of the old chapel guessed at the hour.
It was Christmas Eve.

The scent of rosemary
gifted the cold air and he felt his heart
lift with a *joie de vivre*
that had made his art the world's exuberant twin —
everything to win.

The dog cartooned for home,
Le Mas Notre-Dame-de-Vie; the chauffeur
smoked by the Oldsmobile,
the lamps of Mougins whispering on below
and a daub of moon.

Then the Maestro was there,
grinning, rubbing his hands, as the dog barked
and they jumped in the back;
only a goat munching the grass seeing them leave
in the pastel dusk.

Down the labyrinth lanes
went the Minotaur, as the olive groves
engraved their silvered ghosts.
His eyes were the eyes of God, the eyes of an owl,
widening for Mougins.

So Picasso and dog
entered the bar at the top of town,
while the chauffeur brought in
a bag of crayons, brushes and paints from the car
and the drinkers clapped.

Firstly, he drew his glass
on the tablecloth, then crayoned the wine,
the glow of its beige pink;
the bottle, its *Torch of Medusa* lines and curves
beautifully female.

Even lovelier though,
the barmaid resting her chin on her arms,
accepting his strong gaze
as he sketched her face, tousling her ebony hair
with a smudge of thumb.

The proprietor came
with olives and canapés. He drew them.
A thin musician played
a carol. He drew him; wooing his plump guitar,
smitten with music.

Allez! He stood to go,
So did they all – le boucher, boulanger,
le fabricant de chandelier
dispersing red candles from each of his pockets
to burn and follow.

The hills giggled in light
across the valley; the mountains scumbled
with snow; and Picasso
led the fervent procession up to the Town Square;
the Christmas Tree there.

Outside at the cafe,
he painted plates – anointed them owls,
bulls, boys, girls, Spanish suns.
And the town choir sang by the mirthful tree, praising
his pure alchemy.

Give us a warm fire, Lord.
Alegre, Alegre, God give us joy.
Noël – all will be blessed.
And if this coming year there are no more of us,
may there be no less.

Then to *Le Feu Follet*
for a feast, where, sipping aperitifs
facing the small Town Hall,
Picasso leapt up to paint the dove of peace
on its honeyed wall.

Shooting stars! He toasted
Cézanne, Van Gogh, Apollinaire – *mes frères* –
while from the restaurant
the accordion player squeezed *La Vie en Rose*
then Picasso chose:

a lobster, which frightened
the curious restaurant cat; blue claws
snapping the air, mad clack
on the plate as Picasso slashed with his crayons
and captured it whole;

then twelve oysters on ice,
which reminded him of his friend Matisse;
how he painted the smell
painted the taste of the ocean's flesh in the mouth.
And this made him smile.

A boy in a white shirt,
shy, came to Picasso's table and bowed
and Monsieur Picasso
painted an octopus on his shirt, both long sleeves
dangling in water.

More! He folded and tore
then unfolded the paper tablecloth —
voilà! – held it aloft,
transformed into friezes of dancers and dogs
and all took a scrap.

He drew the maître d',
the sommelier and his wife, the chef,
the waiters, the diners
and, old man in the mirror there, washing his hands,
his last self-portrait.

He sketched from the church steps
as the townsfolk carolled to midnight mass
and he drew against death,
the ending of light; watching a boy lead a lamb
to the Christmas hour.

Then he left his great gifts,
climbed in the dark waiting car with his dog,
eyes priming the blank moon.
Mes enfants, remember the Noël Picasso
drew, painted the town.

FROST FAIR

So cold it was:
by late December, ink had frosted
in its well; my breath was tinkling
on my lips, so everything I saw to tell
I had to memorise. I saw birds
fall from trees, too stiff to fly, like stones.
I saw a lass, her tongue stuck to a spoon.
I saw an ice-hare staring lifeless at no moon.

All this as I walked from Spitalfields
by way of London Bridge to Southwark, dressed
as a man for reasons of my own; a poet-spy;
Anon. At Bishopsgate, I fell in with a crowd
all streaming south. I saw a frozen cat
arched on a wall; a lad kicking a silvered rat;
and not one chilly citizen could doff his hat.

London was snow. St Paul's, a talent of the snow
to seem more grand. The bells hung in their towers,
dumb. Trees went to pieces; cracked. Men's tears
were jewels in their beards for wives to pluck.
I saw a spider's web enriched with rime.
I saw a clock too cold to tell the time;
a pickpocket's hand too blue to do the crime.

The air more cruel, it nipped and bit me
to a tavern, where I ordered up mulled wine
and listened in. A sailor spoke of how the sea
lay fettered to the shore. A sad-faced jester
warmed his chittering monkey at the fire.
I saw a barefoot vagrant enter, pale
as death, and beg for bread, and fail.
I saw the monkey sink a pint of ale.

At Billingsgate, fishwives threw fistfights
and the fishermen were drunk as eels;
the empty nets heaped in their frigid chains.
One wailed his boat was crushed to sticks.
One swore he'd spied a dolphin, turned to lead
upon a moveless wave; so help him God.
I saw him charge a crown for a cod.

I mused on climate – how it could clench
the greatest city in its bitter fist
and squeeze. For now I stood on London Bridge,
next to a man with walrus for a face,
beside a bawd whose eyes were hard as gems.
My mouth as wide as one at Bethlehem's,
I saw another town on the Thames.

Where men had drowned, there stretched
whole streets of booths. A coach and six drove down
the central avenue. Folk slid and skated
on the ice. Large boats were drawn by mules.
Tents waved with flags. I saw a bear
surrounded by a boozy mob; by Temple Stairs,
jugglers on stilts proclaimed a travelling fair.

I walked on water; heard my steps click
on its thickened back; slipped on my arse.
Vendors sold gingerbread, black pudding, snuff,
plum cake, brandy balls, hot pudding, pies.
I found a Fuddling Tent and drank spiced rum.
I saw a wheeled boat with a youth banging a drum.
I saw a fox-hunt; fire-eater; football scrum.

I met a wench who thought I was a man,
or didn't care, and stole a salty kiss.
I've never seen her since. I tossed a coin
to watch a man swallow his sword. I paid a sixpence
to a printer for my name, the place, the date, the year,
to truly certify that I was here.
I saw a piglet roasted on a spear.

And everywhere, a vital human thrum
as if no one would ever die; the wild faces
of a carnival, all in their cups; mad freedom
from the usual. I saw a couple married
by a tipsy priest, exchanging rings of ice
carved by a silversmith. I bought a necklace
on a whim, which didn't melt till Candlemas.

The frail shy sun, a cloistered nun, faded
and vanished. The river was the moon's
to flatter more; embellish upheaved floes
to crystal walls; sparkle St Paul's.
I saw a hundred dancing fires lit.
I saw a whole ox turning on a spit
and swapped a shilling for a steaming slice of it.

I skidded to a fortune-teller's booth
and had my palm read there by candlelight.
The one-eyed dame squinted my love and luck.
To celebrate, I took up with a group of players,
who sang and passed round brandy in a ring:
And folk do tipple without fear to sink
More liquor than the fish beneath do drink.

We stole the blankets which made up a shop;
laid out rough beds. And so it was, I slept
a whole night on the Thames, between
a farting Friar and a snoring Juliet.
I'm aching yet. I limp. I woke at dawn.
I saw the King upon the bridge, staring down;
a cap of glittering stalagmites for a crown.

Time to move on. The King had disappeared
when I climbed the bridge and made my eyes
commit a wonder to my heart. Two swans
alighted, swerving on the blazing glaze,
then flew, creaking, away. I spoke a prayer.
I saw my words freeze on the air
and hang, preserved, to thaw now in your ear.